Dear Parents and Educc

Welcome to Penguin Yo ucators, you know that each child de in terms of speech, critical thinking uin Young Readers recognizes this fact. As a result, each Penguin Young Readers book is assigned a traditional easy-to-read level (1–4) as well as a Guided Reading Level (A–P). Both of these systems will help you choose the right book for your child. Please refer to the back of each book for specific leveling information. Penguin Young Readers features esteemed authors and illustrators, stories about favorite characters, fascinating nonfiction, and more!

Young Cam Jansen and the Molly Shoe Mystery

LEVEL 3

GUIDED READING LEVEL J

This book is perfect for a **Transitional Reader** who:

- can read multisyllable and compound words;
- can read words with prefixes and suffixes;
- is able to identify story elements (beginning, middle, end, plot, setting, characters, problem, solution); and
- can understand different points of view.

Here are some **activities** you can do during and after reading this book:

- Character Traits: Cam's aunt Molly is a very interesting character. Write down a list of words to describe her.
- Setting: The setting of a story is where it takes place. Discuss the setting in this story. (There might be more than one!) Use evidence from the text to describe it.
- Make Connections: Have you ever lost something? Talk about what it was and what you did to find it.

Remember, sharing the love of reading with a child is the best gift you can give!

—Bonnie Bader, EdM
Penguin Young Readers program

*Penguin Young Readers are leveled by independent reviewers applying the standards developed by Irene Fountas and Gay Su Pinnell in *Matching Books to Readers: Using Leveled Books in Guided Reading*, Heinemann, 1999.

For Natalie Grace Zellner—
happy reading—DA

To Uncle Bill—SN

Penguin Young Readers
Published by the Penguin Group
Penguin Group (USA) Inc., 375 Hudson Street, New York, New York 10014, USA
Penguin Group (Canada), 90 Eglinton Avenue East, Suite 700, Toronto, Ontario M4P 2Y3, Canada
(a division of Pearson Penguin Canada Inc.)
Penguin Books Ltd, 80 Strand, London WC2R 0RL, England
Penguin Ireland, 25 St Stephen's Green, Dublin 2, Ireland (a division of Penguin Books Ltd)
Penguin Group (Australia), 707 Collins Street, Melbourne, Victoria 3008, Australia
(a division of Pearson Australia Group Pty Ltd)
Penguin Books India Pvt Ltd, 11 Community Centre, Panchsheel Park, New Delhi—110 017, India
Penguin Group (NZ), 67 Apollo Drive, Rosedale, Auckland 0632, New Zealand
(a division of Pearson New Zealand Ltd)
Penguin Books, Rosebank Office Park, 181 Jan Smuts Avenue, Parktown North 2193, South Africa
Penguin China, B7 Jaiming Center, 27 East Third Ring Road North,
Chaoyang District, Beijing 100020, China

Penguin Books Ltd, Registered Offices: 80 Strand, London WC2R 0RL, England

 First published in 2008 by Viking and in 2009 by Puffin Books, imprints of Penguin Group (USA) Inc. Published in 2013 by Penguin Young Readers, an imprint of Penguin Group (USA) Inc., 345 Hudson Street, New York, New York 10014. Manufactured in China.

The Library of Congress has cataloged the Viking edition
under the following Control Number: 2007031181

ISBN 978-0-14-241402-6 10 9 8 7 6 5 4 3

PENGUIN YOUNG READERS

LEVEL 3
TRANSITIONAL READER

Young Cam Jansen
and the Molly Shoe Mystery

by David A. Adler
illustrated by Susanna Natti

Penguin Young Readers
An Imprint of Penguin Group (USA) Inc.

Contents

Chapter 1
Aunt Molly Quacks

"I like your aunt Molly,"

Eric Shelton told his friend

Cam Jansen.

"She's so funny.

Once, I said hello to

her and she said, 'Quack!'"

"Molly works for an airline,"

Cam's father said.

"She flies so much

that sometimes she feels like a duck."

Cam, Eric, and Cam's father
were on their way to the airport.
Aunt Molly was coming to visit,
and they were picking her up.
Cam's father parked his car.
"We're late," he said.
He hurried through the parking lot.
Cam and Eric followed him.
Mr. Jansen stopped by the door
to the arrivals building.
"Oh my," he said.

He turned and looked

at all the cars in the parking lot.

"I already forgot

where I parked our car."

"I remember," Cam said.

Cam closed her eyes and said, "Click!"

Then, with her eyes closed, she said,

"Our car is in section E4.

It's parked between a red car

and a blue van."

Cam's memory is like a camera.

"I have pictures in my head

of whatever I've seen," Cam says.

"*Click!* is the sound my camera makes."

Cam's real name is Jennifer.

But because of her amazing memory,

people started calling her

"the Camera."

Soon "the Camera" became

just "Cam."

"Good," Mr. Jansen said.

"Now let's find Aunt Molly."

Chapter 2
"I Know You"

Cam opened her eyes.

She and Eric followed Cam's father

into the building.

Just inside, the sun was shining

through many large windows.

"I'm sorry," Eric said.

"The sun is in my eyes.

I can't see, so I can't find Aunt Molly."

“Shade them,” Mr. Jansen said.

Mr. Jansen held his hand

above his eyes.

Cam and Eric shaded their eyes, too.

They looked across the large room.

Along one side were small shops

selling newspapers, candies,

flowers, and balloons.

In the middle were chairs.

The chairs on one side of the room,

the side in the sun, were empty.

The shaded side of the room

was crowded.

"There she is," Eric said.

He hurried across the room.

He stopped by a woman
who was reading.
Eric said, “Hello, Aunt Molly.”
The woman looked up.
“Oh,” Eric said.
“You’re not Aunt Molly.”
The woman laughed.
Eric looked for Cam.
She was with her father.
They were talking to someone.

"Oh, there she is!" Eric said.

Eric hurried to Cam.

"I'm a tired duck," Aunt Molly said.

She rubbed her eyes.

"I wanted to stretch across a few chairs, but this side of the room is too crowded," she said.

Mr. Jansen asked, "What about the other side?"

"That's too sunny," Aunt Molly told him.

"I tried, but I couldn't rest."

“Let’s go,” Mr. Jansen said.

“You can rest at home.”

“Hey,” Aunt Molly said to Eric.

“I know you.

You’re Cam’s friend, Elroy.”

“I’m not Elroy,” Eric said.

“Leroy?”

Eric shook his head.

“My name is Eric Shelton.”

“Oh, hello, Sheldon.

I’m Molly Jansen.”

Cam laughed and said,

"Hello, Leroy Sheldon."

Eric and Mr. Jansen laughed, too.

Aunt Molly got up

and started toward the door.

"What about your suitcase?"

Mr. Jansen asked.

"And what about your shoes?"

Cam asked.

Aunt Molly looked down.

"Oh my," she said.

"I'm not wearing them."

Chapter 3
China, Chile, and Peru

"Hey," Aunt Molly said.

"I'm wearing pretty socks."

She wriggled her toes.

"But where are my shoes?

They're my favorites.

They're red with shiny gold buckles.

They were made for me in London."

Aunt Molly turned to Eric and said,

"You know, Sheldon,

that's a long way from here.

It’s a big city in another country.”
Aunt Molly smiled and told Eric,
“Call me if you want to go to London.
I sell airline tickets.”
“Molly,” Mr. Jansen asked,
“where are your shoes?”
Aunt Molly looked down again.
She wriggled her toes and said,
“I don’t know.”

Eric said, “Some people take their shoes off when they rest.”

“That’s what I do,”
Aunt Molly told him.

“I’ll look for them,” Cam said.

Cam went back to where
Aunt Molly had been resting.
She looked under the chair.
Then she hurried back.

“I found these coins,” Cam said.

“But I didn’t find your shoes.”

“Oh,” Aunt Molly said.

“The coins dropped from my pocket.

I brought them for you.

They’re from different countries—

from China, Chile, and Peru.

Please share them with Sheldon.”

Cam kept a few coins.

She gave a few to Eric.

"Thank you," Eric said.

Then he asked Aunt Molly,

"Did you rest on the airplane?"

"Yes, I always do."

"Then that's where your shoes are,"

Eric said.

"You left them on the airplane."

Chapter 4
Pebbles and Puddles

"Maybe I did leave them there,"
Aunt Molly said.
Mr. Jansen said, "Let's go back and
look for them."
Aunt Molly's suitcase had wheels.
She pulled it through the terminal.
Cam, Eric, and Mr. Jansen followed
her to the airline's information desk.
"Hi, I'm Molly Jansen,"
Aunt Molly said.
"I was on flight number . . .
What flight was I on?"

"I know,"
Cam said.
"You sent us
an e-mail."

Cam closed her eyes.
She said, "Click!" and looked at the
picture in her head.
"You were on flight 72."
Molly told the man behind the desk,
"I think I left my favorite shoes
on flight 72.
They're red with shiny gold buckles."
"I'll check," the man said.
He made a telephone call.
He waited and then shook his head.
Her shoes were not on the airplane.

Aunt Molly slowly pulled her suitcase

toward the door.

"I loved those shoes," she said.

Aunt Molly didn't look

where she was walking.

She stepped into a puddle

of spilled soda.

"Now my socks are wet!"

Aunt Molly sat down.

"I need my suitcase," she said.

"I have to change my socks."

"Hey," Cam said.

"There's a lump in your suitcase.

Maybe that lump is your shoes.

Maybe when you rested,

you put your shoes in your suitcase."

Aunt Molly opened her suitcase.

"Look," she said.

"It's cheddar cheese!"

Aunt Molly took out

a large wrapped block of cheese.

She took out a box of crackers.

"I love cheese and crackers," she said.

"Who wants some?"

"What about your socks?"

Mr. Jansen asked.

Aunt Molly found a pair of socks

in her suitcase.

She put them on.

She didn't find her shoes.

"I'll go without shoes,"

Aunt Molly said.

"I'll just look out for

puddles and pebbles."

Aunt Molly started toward the door.
Cam, Eric, and Mr. Jansen
followed her.
When Aunt Molly got near the door,
she shaded her eyes.
Cam stopped.
Cam looked at the sun
shining through the windows
She looked at Aunt Molly.
"Wait!" Cam said.
"I think I know where
to find your shoes.
I think I solved the mystery."

Chapter 5
"Let's Go Home"

"That's great!" Aunt Molly said.
"Now let's go home."
"First let's see if Cam can find
your shoes," Eric said.
Cam and Eric went back to the
sunny side of the room.
Cam said, "When Aunt Molly shaded
her eyes, I remembered that she
tried to rest here.
It was too sunny, so she moved.
Maybe she left her shoes here."

Cam and Eric looked
under the chairs.
They found newspapers
and paper cups.
Then Eric reached under a chair
and pulled out a pair of shoes.
They were red with shiny gold buckles.

Eric brought the shoes to Aunt Molly.

"Are these yours?" he asked.

"Yes," Aunt Molly said.

Aunt Molly put the shoes on.

"Thank you," Aunt Molly said.

"Now let's go home."

Aunt Molly walked toward the door.

"Molly!" Mr. Jansen said.

"You forgot your suitcase."

Mr. Jansen pulled the suitcase
toward the door.
Then he stopped.
"Oh my," he said.
"With all this talk of shoes,
I forgot where I parked the car."
Eric said, "I'm sure Cam remembers."
Cam closed her eyes and said, "Click!"
"The car is in E4," Cam said.
Cam opened her eyes.
"Let's go," Mr. Jansen said.
"Before we forget something else."
"Yes," Aunt Molly said.
"This tired duck needs to rest."

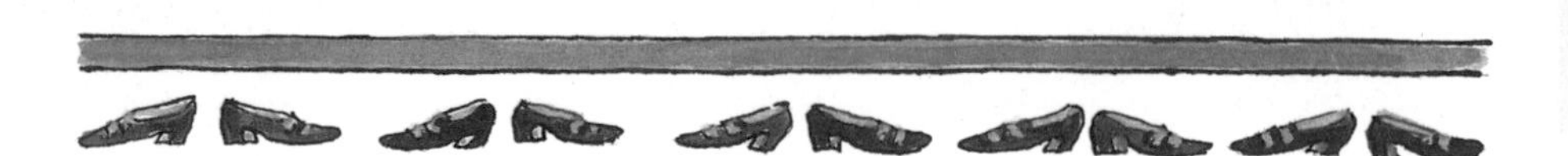

A Cam Jansen Memory Game

Take another look at the picture on page 31.
Study it.
Blink your eyes and say, "Click!"
Then turn back to this page
and answer these questions:

1. Are there more than eight people in the picture?
2. What color are Cam's pants? What color are Eric's?
3. Is Cam wearing a jacket?
4. Is anyone pushing a luggage cart?
5. Is Cam smiling? Is Eric?